Storm
the Lightning
Fairy

To Abby and Becky French
– with lots of love

Special thanks to
Sue Mongredien

No part of this work may be reproduced, stored in a retrieval system, or transmitted in any form or by any means, electronic, mechanical, photocopying, recording, or otherwise, without written permission of the publisher. For information regarding permission, write to Rainbow Magic Limited, c/o HIT Entertainment, 830 South Greenville Avenue, Allen, TX 75002-3320.

ISBN-13: 978-0-439-81391-4
ISBN-10: 0-439-81391-3

14   13 14/0

Printed in the U.S.A.   40

Storm
the Lightning
Fairy

by Daisy Meadows

SCHOLASTIC INC.

New York   Toronto   London   Auckland   Sydney
Mexico City   New Delhi   Hong Kong   Buenos Aires

The Fairyland Palace

Forest of

Candy Factory

The Village Hall

River

Wetherbury Village

Far

Jack Frost's
Ice Castle

reen Wood

Mrs. Fordham's House

The Park

Willow Hill

High St.

The Museum

irsty's
House

Fields

Mudhole

N
W — E
S

Goblins green and goblins small,
I cast this spell to make you tall.
As high as the palace you shall grow.
My icy magic makes it so.

Then steal the rooster's magic feathers,
used by the fairies to make all weathers.
Climate chaos I have planned
on Earth, and here, in Fairyland!

Contents

Magic in the Air

"I can't believe tomorrow is my last day here," groaned Rachel Walker. She was staying with her friend, Kirsty Tate, in Wetherbury for a week. The girls had gone on so many adventures together, they knew it was going to be hard to say good-bye.

Now, they were walking to the park,

excited to be outside. It had been pouring rain all night, but now the sun was shining again.

"Put on your coats, please," Mrs. Tate had told them before they left. "It looks awfully breezy out there!"

"It's been so much fun having you visit," Kirsty told her friend. "I don't think I'll ever forget this week. Will you?" Rachel shook her head. "No way," she agreed.

The two friends smiled at each other. It had been a very busy week. A snowy, windy, cloudy, sunny, misty week — thanks to Jack Frost and his goblins. The goblins had stolen the seven magic tail feathers from Doodle, Fairyland's weather rooster. The Weather Fairies used the feathers to control the weather, so now that the goblins had them, they were stirring up all kinds of trouble!

Rachel and Kirsty were helping the Weather Fairies get the feathers back. Without them, Doodle was just an ordinary weather vane! Kirsty's dad had found it lying in the park. He brought it home and put it on the roof of their old barn.

"Doodle has five of his magic feathers back now. I hope we find the last two before you have to go home," Kirsty said, pushing open the park gate.

Rachel nodded, but before she could say anything, raindrops started splashing down around them.

The girls looked up to see a huge purple storm cloud covering the sun. The sky was getting darker by the second, and the rain was coming down harder and harder.

"Run, quick!" Kirsty shouted. "Before we get soaked!"

The girls started to run, and Rachel put her hands over her head as raindrops poured down from above. It was raining so hard that she could hardly see the path ahead. "Where are we going?" she cried.

"Let's just find some place out of the rain," Kirsty replied, grabbing Rachel's hand. "I'm soaked already!" The girls stopped under a big chestnut tree near the park entrance. The tree's wide, leafy branches were perfect for keeping away the rain. "Great idea," said Rachel, shivering and trying to shake the raindrops off her coat.

Just as she said that, there was a loud

clap of thunder, followed by a bright
flash! The whole sky lit up with a bolt of
lightning.

Kirsty and Rachel watched in shock as
the lightning bolt slammed right into the
chestnut tree.

"We need to get away from here!" Kirsty cried, jumping back in fright. "It's dangerous being under a tree during a thunderstorm!"

"Wait a minute," Rachel said, staring up at a tree branch. Rain was pouring off her shoulders, but she didn't seem to notice. "Kirsty, look. That branch is *sparkling*."

And it was! The leaves were glittering green, glowing through the dark storm.

Tiny twinkling lights flickered all over the branch. It reminded Kirsty of the trees they'd seen in Fairyland. They almost seemed to sparkle with fairy dust! And that made her think that maybe . . .

"It's a *magical* storm!" Kirsty exclaimed, her eyes almost as bright as the shining leaves. "Look at the sky, Rachel!"

Both girls looked up in wonder as the lightning flashed again. A million sparkling lights danced around the thunderclouds, then faded away into the darkness.

Rachel grinned with excitement. "It's magical, but very wet!" she said, laughing. "Let's find somewhere drier and safer. Come on!"

The Fairy Storm

Rachel and Kirsty ran out of the park and back to the road. The rain was still pouring down, sticking their hair against their heads. It was so dark and wet out that all of the cars driving past had their headlights on and their windshield wipers whipping from side to side.

Instead of running all the way home,

Kirsty had another idea. "Let's go in there!" she cried, pointing ahead.

Rachel blinked the raindrops from her eyelashes and followed her friend up the path to a large red brick building. A small blue sign out front read: WETHERBURY MUSEUM.

Kirsty yanked open
the double doors,
and she and Rachel
tumbled inside the
museum. Water
dripped onto the
doormat as Rachel
shook her hair out
of her face.

"Wow!" she said.
"Talk about stormy weather!"

Kirsty looked thoughtful. "The goblin
with the Lightning Feather must be
behind this," she said. "He's nearby,
don't you think?"

"Definitely," Rachel agreed. "I—"

But before she could say anything else,
Rachel was interrupted by a deafening
ROOOAAARRR!

Rachel clutched Kirsty's arm. "What was that?" she whispered.

Kirsty giggled at her friend's alarmed face. "I should have warned you — there's  a dinosaur display in here," she said. "They found some dinosaur bones in Wetherbury years and years ago. The museum has a huge model of how the dinosaur would have looked. It roars and moves every few minutes. Come on, I'll show you."

Kirsty pushed open another set of double doors and led Rachel into one of the museum galleries. A group of people was being shown around by a tour guide.

Kirsty pointed past them to a gigantic
model dinosaur.

Rachel stared at the long neck, wide
body, and huge tail of the model. The
dinosaur was standing in water that was

supposed to look like a river. Spiky
rubber fish floated around its feet.

"Wow!" Rachel exclaimed.

Kirsty grinned. "Watch this," she said,
pressing a big red button.

The dinosaur leaned down and opened

its jaws. It snapped up one of the fish, then lifted its head so that the fish tumbled down into its belly. "That's amazing!" Rachel said, laughing. "What happens if you press this blue button?"

RROOOOOAAARRRR!

"That's what happens," Kirsty giggled.

As the dinosaur's roar faded, Rachel couldn't help overhearing the tour guide. "Listen!" she whispered to Kirsty. ". . . don't know where this fairy exhibit has come from," the guide was saying, sounding confused. She shrugged. "I just came back from vacation — it must be a new display. Maybe somebody discovered that fairies were around at the same time as dinosaurs!" The tour group laughed politely. "Anyway, let's move on to the

18

natural history room," the guide said. "It's this way. . . ."

Rachel and Kirsty crept to the back of the tour group to check out the fairy exhibit. If they stood on their tiptoes, the girls could see over all the heads to one of the display cases. There seemed to be a tiny shape in there, but they couldn't tell what it was from so far away.

As the group followed the tour guide out of the room, there was another loud growl of thunder. The girls saw a dazzling flash of lightning through the

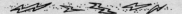

windows. Once again, the sky seemed to glitter with silver sparkles. Then all the lights went out inside the museum.

"Oh, dear, it's a power outage," the

guide said, sighing, as her tour group gasped. "Follow me, everyone — I think we have some flashlights over here."

Rachel and Kirsty waited until the group had left the room, then went to take a closer look at the fairy display case. Inside was a real, live fairy, glowing with magic — and she was waving frantically at them!

Rachel in Danger

"It's Storm the Lightning Fairy!" cried Rachel, hurrying to open the case. She found a tiny hook on the side and unlatched it so that the glass door swung open.

"Hello, again," said Storm. "I'm so glad to see you two!"

Rachel and Kirsty had met all the

Weather Fairies at the beginning of their feather-finding mission. The King and Queen of Fairyland had brought the girls to Fairyland to ask for their help, so now they recognized the fairy right away. Storm had long, straight blonde hair and wore a bright purple outfit. A golden lightning bolt hung on a chain around her neck, and her purple wand sent out little crackling lightning bolts whenever it moved.

"Hello, Storm!" said Kirsty, as the fairy fluttered out of the glass case. "I was wondering when we were going to see you. What were you doing in there?"

Storm tossed her hair. "The goblin with the Lightning Feather trapped me in there," she explained, annoyed. "He's still somewhere in the museum. Have you seen all the lightning he's been making?" She put her hands on her hips. "Please help me get my feather back from him. Lightning is powerful stuff, you know."

"We know," Rachel told her. "We were under a tree when lightning struck. One of the branches broke!"

Storm looked horrified, so Kirsty tried to make her feel better. "It was very pretty lightning, though, Storm," she said. "All sparkly!"

Storm smiled. "It is beautiful, isn't it?" she said. Then she sighed. "But I have to get the feather back before that mean goblin does any more damage. Those goblins have no idea —" Storm broke off in the middle of her sentence. "Someone's coming," she whispered. "It might be the goblin. Hide!"

The girls pressed themselves back against the wall and Storm swooped down onto Kirsty's shoulder. They were half-hidden by a display case in the darkness. Thunder rumbled again, and Kirsty realized that her heart was pounding. She really hoped the noise they heard was just the tour guide coming back, not the goblin. Jack Frost had cast a spell to make all the goblins bigger, so now they were almost as tall as the girls' shoulders. That made it even harder for Kirsty and Rachel to get the Weather Feathers back from them!

The door creaked open, and the girls and Storm all held their breath. Through the darkness they could see that it was the goblin. And, he was a particularly scary-looking one — with extra-narrow red eyes, long, pointed ears, and a thin, bony body. The lights were still out in the museum, but the goblin lit up the room. He was waving the Lightning Feather around so that golden bolts of lightning whizzed all over the place. They crackled and fizzed, sending electric blue sparks shooting from everything they touched. Storm put her head in her hands. "I can't watch," she groaned. "What does he think he's doing?"

"Oh!" gasped Rachel, ducking as a lightning bolt zoomed past her head. "We have to stop him before he hurts someone," she hissed.

"Who said that?" the goblin snapped.
"Fairy, was that you? Or is somebody
else in here?"

Kirsty's heart pounded so loudly that
she was sure the goblin would hear it. He
was turning around, looking everywhere
to see who'd made the noise. At last, his
red eyes fell upon the girls, and he grinned
a horrible grin.

"Oh!" he cried. "Planning to sneak up

on me, were you?" And with a wave of the feather, he sent three fiery lightning bolts whizzing right at them!

"Duck!" cried Storm, diving into Kirsty's coat pocket. The girls threw themselves behind a display case and the lightning crashed to the ground, only missing them by a few inches. Wisps of glittering smoke rose from a scorch mark on the floor. The smoke drifted up to the ceiling, where it finally fizzled out in a shower of blue sparks like

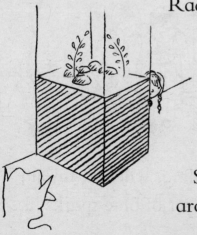

a tiny firework. Fairy lightning was powerful stuff!

"What do we do now?" whispered Kirsty, her face white.

"I don't know," Rachel whispered back. "Storm — do you have any ideas?"

Storm shook her head. "The goblin is holding the feather so tightly, there's no way I can fly over and grab it," she said, frowning.

Rachel bit her lip. They needed a plan — fast! "I'll just peek out to see where he is," she whispered. She poked her head around the side of the display case, only to see the goblin creeping closer to them.

"There you are!" he yelled, and waved the Lightning Feather again.

To Rachel's horror, a lightning bolt came shooting right at her face!

A Wild Idea

Rachel ducked back behind the display case just in time. The lightning bolt whizzed so close to her, it burned the edge of her coat.

Storm fluttered up into the air, a determined look on her face. "Shrink to fairy size, girls!" she called. "It'll be harder for him to blast you when you're small."

Kirsty's fingers were shaking so much that she could barely open her fairy locket. The Queen of the Fairies had given her and Rachel one locket each. They were filled with magical fairy dust. Kirsty finally flipped open the lid and sprinkled the dust all over herself. Seconds later, she felt the familiar whooshing. She shrank smaller and smaller until she was the same size as Storm. She shook out her wings and spun in the air. Being a fairy was so much fun!

Rachel looked like a giant next to her. "I can't find my locket," she said anxiously.

Just then, Kirsty spotted it shining on the floor under a display case, out of Rachel's reach. She pointed it out. "It must have fallen off when you ducked for cover!" she said.

Before Kirsty could fly down and grab the locket for her friend, the goblin ran over, closer and closer. He held the Lightning Feather tightly in his hand, and Rachel could see a wicked glint in his eye.

"Help!" she cried, dodging to one side. "Can you distract him, Storm?"

Storm was whizzing through the air, trying to get close enough to Rachel to sprinkle fairy dust onto her, but the goblin was blocking her way. And he was still waving the feather around, sending lightning bolts flashing in every direction. It was too dangerous for Kirsty or Storm to move any closer to Rachel.

"What are we going to do?" Kirsty
yelled as she watched Rachel run from
the goblin. The doors crashed open as
Rachel sprinted into the next room.
Kirsty and Storm flew behind her, not
sure what to do.

The room was full of
animal and insect exhibits.
Luckily, there were no
people around. The tour
group must have headed
for home when the
power went out.

The goblin chased
Rachel past cases of
colorful butterflies,
and then around a
large glass box full of
thousands of bustling ants.

The goblin waved the feather, and a bolt of lightning slammed against the ant house, scattering the ants inside. Kirsty thought her friend had done a great job of escaping the goblin so far, but she knew Rachel couldn't keep it up forever. She had to think of some way to help!

Kirsty racked her brains as she and Storm followed Rachel and the

goblin back into the dinosaur room.
Suddenly, she spotted a large mirror
hanging on one wall. An idea came to
her. A crazy idea. A wild idea! But, she
thought, it might just work. . . .

Kirsty to the Rescue

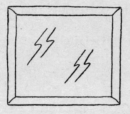

Kirsty pointed up at the mirror. "Would lightning be strong enough to break that?" she asked Storm quickly.

Storm shook her head. "No, fairy lightning isn't like normal lightning. It would just bounce back off a mirror," she replied.

Kirsty grinned. "Perfect," she said. "I'm

going to try to surprise the goblin. You get ready to grab the feather!"

Kirsty could tell that Rachel was starting to get tired, so she flew down toward the goblin right away. He was just stretching out a bony hand to grab Rachel's coat, when Kirsty tugged hard on one of his long ears.

"Ow! Who did that?" he yelped, jumping back.

Kirsty fluttered up in front of the mirror. "Yoo-hoo! Over here!" she yelled, waving. "Catch me if you can!"

She saw the goblin aim the Lightning Feather right at her. "Silly little fairy," he yelled. "Take that!" And another crackling, golden lightning bolt zoomed toward Kirsty.

Kirsty held her breath as she watched it whiz through the air. It was so close, she could almost feel its heat on her face!

"Move!" Rachel shouted in panic, terrified that her friend was going to get hit.

But Kirsty waited until the very last second. Then, just as the lightning was about to strike her, she dodged out of its way. The fairy lightning struck the mirror and, as Storm had predicted, it

bounced right back — straight at the goblin!

"Help!" he shouted, trying to get out of the way. He tripped over his own big feet and fell to the ground under the dinosaur model, dropping the Lightning Feather!

Quick as a flash, Storm was there, diving toward the feather in a blur of purple and gold. She snatched it up and flew high in the air, out of the reach of

goblin fingers. "Nice work, Kirsty!" she
cheered.

"Hey!" yelled the goblin in fury,
jumping up to try to reach the feather.
He fell awkwardly against the dinosaur,

lost his balance, and tumbled right into the water below with the rubber fish!

Grinning mischievously, Storm pointed the Lightning Feather at the model dinosaur. A stream of fiery lightning bolts shot out of the feather and struck the red and blue buttons on the control panel. Rachel's eyes widened as the dinosaur sparkled all over for a second, and then . . .

"*RROOOOAAARRRRRR!*" And with that, the dinosaur bent down and snatched up the goblin in its teeth!

Doodle's Warning

Rachel, Kirsty, and Storm watched in amazement as the dinosaur lifted up its head with the struggling goblin still in its mouth.

"Put me down!" the goblin cried. "*Aaaaargghh!*"

Of course, the model didn't listen to the goblin but just went through its usual

process. It tipped its head back, opened
its jaws a little wider, and . . . *clatter, clunk,
bang, bang, crash*! The goblin

tumbled right down
into the dinosaur's
hollow belly! A
furious pounding
started inside
the model.
"Let me out!"
yelled the goblin.
Laughing with delight, Kirsty
sprinkled another pinch of fairy
dust over herself. It glittered bright white.
Then she felt her wings disappear and her
legs grow and — *WHOOSH!* — she was
back to being a regular-sized girl again.

She ran to Rachel and hugged her.

"Are you OK?" she asked. "That was scary, wasn't it?"

"Yes," Rachel agreed. "But everything turned out fine, thanks to your great idea, Kirsty. Now we have Doodle's sixth feather back!"

Storm flew over to the girls with Rachel's

magical locket in her hands. "Here you go," she said, handing it over. "I think we'd better leave while we can," she added nervously. "It sounds like the goblin's trying to climb out of the dinosaur. It won't take him long to escape and tell Jack Frost what's happened!" They could all hear the determined scratching sounds that were coming from inside the dinosaur.

Rachel fastened her locket carefully around her neck as the three friends headed for the museum's exit. "I can't believe I missed out on being a fairy today," she said with a sigh. "That's the only bad part. That — and almost getting zapped by fairy lightning!" she finished with a smile.

Outside, the rain had stopped and the dark clouds seemed to be melting away. The sun came out and made the wet pavement sparkle.

Rachel glanced down and groaned. "Oh, no," she said. "My coat! I forgot that it got burned by the goblin's lightning."

Kirsty looked over as Rachel pulled up her coat to examine it. The material was black and scorched, and the stitching had fizzled away.

"Mom's going to be upset," Rachel said. "This coat was supposed to last through the new school year!"

"Let me see," said Storm, darting down

for a closer look. As soon as she saw
the problem, she
smiled and gently
waved her magic
wand along the hem.
A trail of twinkling
lights fell over the
material, and
Rachel gasped as the burned
part of her coat started
shimmering with a bright white
light.

She blinked in the dazzling fairy
glow and, when she looked again, she
saw that her coat was as good as new!
"Thank you, Storm," Rachel gasped in
delight. "Now Mom will never know!"

Storm winked. "I should be the one

thanking you two," she said. "Doodle will be so happy to have another feather back in his tail!"

They hurried down Twisty Lane to Kirsty's house. "There's Doodle," Kirsty told Storm, pointing to the weather vane on top of the old barn.

Storm flew up to
return the Lightning
Feather to Doodle's
tail, and the girls
waited expectantly.
What was Doodle
going to say this
time? Every time
they had put a
feather back before,
the rusty old
weather vane had
magically come alive,
just for a second, and
squawked out part of a
message. So far, he had said,
"Beware! Jack Frost will come if his . . ."
The two friends couldn't wait to find out

what Doodle was going to say next. Jack Frost would come if his . . . *what*?

As Storm carefully put the Lightning Feather into place, Doodle's iron feathers softened and shimmered with a thousand fiery colors. His head turned toward the girls and his beak opened. ". . . goblins fail!" he squawked urgently. Then, just as quickly, the color vanished from Doodle's feathers, his head turned back with a rusty creak, and he was an ordinary weather vane again.

Rachel and Kirsty looked at each other. "Beware! Jack Frost will come if his goblins fail!" they cried together.

Storm looked worried. "If you find the Rain Feather, then Jack Frost's goblins will have failed," she said. "That doesn't sound good." She fluttered down to Kirsty and Rachel. "You must be careful, girls. Jack Frost is very sneaky."

"We know," Kirsty said, biting her lip. "But we'll be careful. Don't worry, Storm."

Kirsty and Rachel hugged Storm goodbye. They watched as the Lightning

Fairy flew into the distance, until she was nothing but a purple sparkle in the air. Then she was gone.

The girls stood in silence for a minute, both thinking about Doodle's warning. Rachel was the first to speak.

"We've almost done it, Kirsty," she said. "But I think the last feather might be the hardest one to get back."

Kirsty nodded. "And even if we do get

it, I'm not looking forward to seeing Jack Frost at all," she said. Then she squeezed Rachel's hand. "But we've  outwitted him before, haven't we? I'm sure we can do it again."

Rachel grinned. "You bet," she agreed. "Watch out, Jack Frost! We're ready for you!" she shouted.

RAINBOW magic™

THE WEATHER FAIRIES

Crystal, Abigail, Pearl, Goldie, Evie, and Storm have all tracked down their feathers. Now Rachel and Kirsty only have

Hayley the Rain Fairy

left to help!

Water, Water, Everywhere!

"OK, OK, I'm awake. You can stop ringing now," mumbled Kirsty Tate sleepily. She reached out to turn off her alarm clock. But strangely, the alarm wasn't ringing.

Quack, quack, quack! The noise that had woken her rang through the air again.

Now that Kirsty was awake, she

realized that the sound hadn't been coming from her alarm clock at all. It was coming from outside instead. She jumped out of bed and peeked between the curtains. "Oh!" she cried. There was water rising right up to her windowsill, and a large, brown duck was swimming past, followed by five fluffy ducklings! Kirsty watched as the mother duck fussed around her babies.

It had been raining really hard all night. In the front yard, the grass and flowerbeds had disappeared under the water. Water lapped against the walls of the old barn, and out past the front gate, the street looked like a silvery mirror.

Kirsty rushed over to her best friend, Rachel Walker, who was asleep in the extra bed. Rachel was staying with

Kirsty for a week during her summer vacation. "Wake up, Rachel! You have to see this!" Kirsty said, shaking her friend gently.

Rachel sat up and rubbed her eyes. "What's going on?"

"I think the river must have overflowed. Everything in Wetherbury is flooded!" replied Kirsty.

"Really?" Rachel was wide awake now, eagerly looking out the window. "That's odd," she said, pointing. "The water isn't so deep in the front yard and the street. How can it be right up to your bedroom window at the same time?"

"Maybe it's Weather Fairy magic!" Kirsty gasped, her eyes shining.

"Of course!" Rachel agreed. She knew that fairy magic followed its own rules.

Kirsty and Rachel were special friends of the fairies. The two girls had met during vacation with their parents to Rainspell Island. There, they had helped the seven Rainbow Fairies get home to Fairyland after Jack Frost's spell had cast them out. Now Jack Frost was up to more trouble, and Rachel and Kirsty were on another secret fairy mission, this time with the Weather Fairies.

"Today's the last day of my vacation," Rachel said sadly.

"I know! We have to find the magic Rain Feather today," Kirsty called over her shoulder, as she quickly got dressed. "It's our last chance. At least with all this magical flooding, we know that the goblin who stole the feather isn't far away!"

Just then, there was a tapping noise at the window. "What if that's the goblin?" Rachel whispered nervously. The goblins were mean, and Jack Frost had cast a spell to make them even bigger than usual.

Kirsty put her finger to her lips. "Shh," she warned, edging toward the window. She peeked out, then threw back the curtains with a smile. An elegant white swan was tapping on the window with its beak. And a tiny fairy was sitting on the swan's back, waving at the girls.

"Oh!" Rachel gasped in delight. "It's Hayley the Rain Fairy!"

RAINBOW magic ™

There's Magic in Every Series!

The Rainbow Fairies
The Weather Fairies
The Jewel Fairies
The Pet Fairies
The Fun Day Fairies
The Petal Fairies
The Dance Fairies
The Music Fairies
The Sports Fairies
The Party Fairies
The Ocean Fairies
The Night Fairies
The Magical Animal Fairies
The Princess Fairies
The Superstar Fairies

Read them all!

scholastic.com
rainbowmagiconline.com

HIT entertainment

RMFAIRY7

RAINBOW magic

These activities are magical!

■SCHOLASTIC

www.scholastic.com
www.rainbowmagiconline.com

RMACTIV

hit entertainment